YASMIN
The Zookeeper

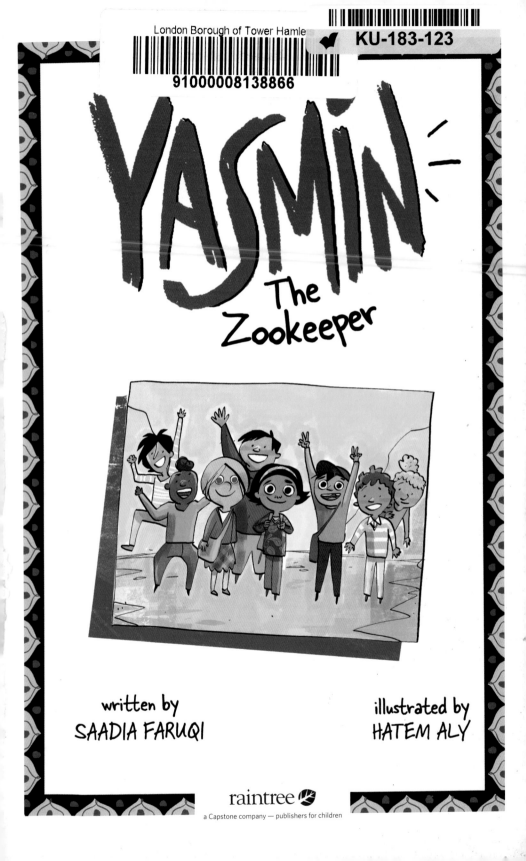

written by
SAADIA FARUQI

illustrated by
HATEM ALY

raintree
a Capstone company — publishers for children

To Mariam for inspiring me, and
Mubashir for helping me find the
right words—S.F.

To my sister, Eman, and her amazing
girls, Jana and Kenzi—H.A.

Raintree is an imprint of Capstone Global Library Limited, a company
incorporated in England and Wales having its registered office at
264 Banbury Road, Oxford, OX2 7DY – Registered company number:
6695582

www.raintree.co.uk
myorders@raintree.co.uk

Text © Capstone Global Library Limited 2020
The moral rights of the proprietor have been asserted.

Edited by Kristen Mohn
Designed by Lori Bye
Original illustrations © Capstone Global Library Limited 2020
Originated by Capstone Global Library Ltd
Printed and bound in India

ISBN 978 1 4747 6974 7
23 22 21
10 9 8 7 6 5 4 3

British Library Cataloguing in Publication Data
A full catalogue record for this book is available from the British Library.

Acknowledgements
Design Elements: Shutterstock: Art and Fashion, rangsan paidaen

TABLE OF CONTENTS

Chapter 1
FIELD TRIP.....................................5

Chapter 2
MEET THE ANIMALS..................11

Chapter 3
HUNGRY MONKEYS....................20

CHAPTER 1

Field trip

Yasmin and Mama walked to school together one morning. At least Mama walked. Yasmin skipped. She was very excited. Today her class was going on a field trip to the zoo.

"Here's your lunch, Yasmin,"
said Mama, handing her a
brown bag. "There's fruit in there
for a snack too."

Yasmin hugged her mother
and boarded the big coach.

Yasmin looked around. She'd never been on a school coach before.

Emma waved to her. "Yasmin, sit with me!"

"Hey, your brown bag is just like mine!" Yasmin said.

"Mine too!" Ali said, popping up behind them. His bag was big! The girls laughed.

"Are you ready, class?" asked Ms Alex.

"Ready!" the children shouted.

The journey to the zoo was very long. The children sang songs and told jokes. Ali's jokes were the funniest.

"What's a kangaroo's favourite game?" he asked.

"Hop Scotch!"

CHAPTER 2

Meet the animals

The zoo was full of all sorts of animals. Ms Alex led the way. First was a pool for seals.

"Look, they're having a bath!" Yasmin said.

A seal swam towards them. It splashed them all with water!

"Don't stand too close," Ms Alex warned. "Remember, this is the animals' home, not yours."

Next they walked to the elephant enclosure. Yasmin counted three elephants: a mama, a baba and a baby.

"How adorable!" cried Emma.

The baba elephant walked

over and snatched Ali's cap from

his head.

"Hey!" shouted Ali. "Give it

back!"

Finally, they reached the

monkey area. *Bandars!* Yasmin's

favourite.

A zookeeper was waiting

for them. "Hello, kids," he said.

"I'm Dave. It's the monkeys'

lunchtime. Would anyone like

to help me?"

All the children put up their hands. Yasmin tried to hold hers up the highest.

"Please pick me," she whispered.

"How about you, in the purple top?" Dave said. He pointed to Yasmin.

"Yes!" Yasmin cheered.

Dave gave Yasmin a big bowl of fruit. It had slices of apples, bananas and oranges.

"Fruit salad!" said Emma.

Yasmin carefully walked towards the monkeys. They squealed and chattered with excitement.

But suddenly, Yasmin tripped!

The bowl of fruit went flying . . .

right into the pond.

CHAPTER 3

Hungry monkeys

The monkeys were upset.
They wanted their lunch! They
screeched and howled. Yasmin's
heart thumped. Would Dave be
angry too?

Then she remembered the
lunch bag in her rucksack.

What had Mama packed?

Yasmin opened it.

A banana!

"Can I share my fruit with the monkeys?" Yasmin asked Dave.

"I suppose it would be all right, just this once," Dave said. He broke the banana into pieces for Yasmin.

A baby monkey climbed onto Yasmin's lap. She held very still as the monkey nibbled banana from her hand. It tickled!

Then Emma took out her brown bag. "I have two oranges," she offered.

The other children took out their brown bags too. Soon all the monkeys had fruit to eat.

"Now it's time for *our* lunch!" Ms Alex said. "Let's go to the playground and eat."

Yasmin waved goodbye to the monkeys.

"Bye, bandars! I'll come again one day, little friends!"

Think about it, talk about it

* Yasmin is a bit nervous about going on a school coach for the first time. How does Emma make Yasmin feel more comfortable? How would you help a friend who felt nervous or scared?

* When Yasmin drops the fruit, she has to think fast to come up with a solution to her problem. Think about a time in your life when something went wrong. What did you do?

* Imagine you are going to a zoo that has every animal in the world. If you could only choose three animals to see, which three would you choose? Why?

Learn Urdu with Yasmin!

Yasmin's family speaks both English and Urdu. Urdu is a language from Pakistan. Perhaps you already know some Urdu words!

baba father

bandar monkey

hijab scarf covering the hair

jaan life; a sweet nickname for a loved one

kameez long tunic or shirt

mama mother

naan flatbread baked in the oven

nana grandfather on mother's side

nani grandmother on mother's side

salaam hello

Pakistan fun facts

Yasmin and her family are proud of their Pakistani culture. Yasmin loves to share facts about Pakistan!

Location

Pakistan is on the continent of Asia, with India on one side and Afghanistan on the other.

Islamabad

PAKISTAN

Population

Pakistan's population is about 207,774,520, making it the world's sixth-most populous country.

National bird

Pakistan's national bird is the chukar, a game bird from the pheasant family.

Zoo

Lahore Zoo in Punjab, Pakistan, is one of the largest zoos in South Asia.

Make a bendy monkey!

YOU WILL NEED:

- construction paper
- scissors
- crayons or felt-tips
- small googly eyes
- glue
- brown and yellow pipe cleaners

STEPS:

1. Cut an oval and a circle from the construction paper to make the monkey's body and head.

2. Glue googly eyes onto the head and draw the rest of the monkey's face. Glue the head to the body.

3. Glue brown pipe cleaners to the back of the body to make the arms and legs. Use another pipe cleaner to make the tail. Make a curl at the tip!

4. To give the monkey a banana, cut and bend a small piece of a yellow pipe cleaner and place it in the monkey's hand.

5. After the glue dries, bend the arms, legs and tail into any pose you choose. Wrap your bendy monkey around a pencil to make a pencil pal!

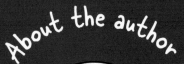

Saadia Faruqi is a Pakistani American writer, interfaith activist and cultural sensitivity trainer previously profiled in *O Magazine*. She is author of the adult short story collection, *Brick Walls: Tales of Hope & Courage from Pakistan*. Her essays have been published in *Huffington Post*, *Upworthy* and *NBC Asian America*. She lives in Texas, USA, with her husband and children.

Hatem Aly is an Egyptian-born illustrator whose work has been featured in multiple publications worldwide. He currently lives in New Brunswick, Canada, with his wife, son and more pets than people. When he is not dipping cookies in a cup of tea or staring at blank pieces of paper, he is usually drawing books. One of the books he illustrated is *The Inquisitor's Tale* by Adam Gidwitz, which won a Newbery Honour and other awards, despite Hatem's drawings of a farting dragon, a two-headed cat and stinky cheese.